FRIDAY'S
TAIL TALE

based on the book by Lois Duncan
screenplay by Jeff Lowell and Bob Schooley & Mark McCorkle

SIMON AND SCHUSTER/NICKELODEON

Based on the movie *Hotel For Dogs*

SIMON AND SCHUSTER

First published in Great Britain in 2009 by Simon and Schuster UK Ltd
1st Floor, 222 Gray's Inn Road, London, WC1X 8HB
A CBS Company

Originally published in the USA in 2009 by Simon Spotlight,
an imprint of Simon & Schuster Children's Publishing Division, New York

A CIP catalogue record for this book is available from the British Library upon request

ISBN: 978 1 84738 568 6

19 9 8 7 6 5 4 3 2 1

Printed in the United Kingdom

Who says a dog's life is easy?
Let me tell you, my life has
been no walk in the park!
I mean, just a few weeks ago
I was roaming the streets
looking for my next meal.
Mmmm . . . I remember that one . . .
lots of yummy MEAT!

Afterwards all I wanted was a
nice, long scratch – but nope!
I can't speak human, but when
my friends Andi and Bruce told me
to "go," I knew I had to leave!
Something smelled funny too.
Either my pals were scared,
or someone needed a bath!

So I waited for my friends
back near their den. They always
made me wait by the window
before letting me inside. Strange!
Sometimes it was not that bad.
Bruce let me sleep with him.
I even had my own fluffy mat!

Their den was fine for sleeping, but their keeper was the worst cook ever! So I had to keep searching the streets for food. One day this human in a uniform looked at me really funny. I knew I had to move again! What is it with humans in uniforms?

Anyway, he caught up with me and picked me up! I had no idea where he was taking me!

Thank goodness my pals saved me!
They are so loyal. But just when
I thought we were safe, we were
on the run – again! But I knew
where we would be safe for sure.
I led and they followed me.

When we got there I could smell
that we were not alone. We had
company, but they were just dogs
like me! One was big and sturdy;
the other was small and fast.

I gave them a quick sniff and
realised they were friendly!
Then we went upstairs to play.
There was a huge bed up there.
I was wiped out, so I took a nice,
long nap with my new friends.

In the next few days my pal
Bruce kept running from room
to room looking for stuff.
It seemed like a fun game, so
I joined in!

Then he started putting things
together and they moved!
Suddenly there were machines everywhere.
There was one that cleaned me –
and it knew all the right spots,
especially my belly!

The big dog liked the gadget
that put pictures on the wall.
And I could rest my paws while
my little friend fetched balls
again and again . . . and again!
I was just happy they both
finally stopped barking.

All of a sudden there were
so many dogs, it was like a play day
in the park that never ended.
Some of the new dogs were dirty,
stinky, and full of fleas – yuck!
Luckily one of the
keepers gave great baths.

Our days were full of things to do.
Some dogs liked to hang their heads
out of this opening and let the air
blow on them. If I got too close I
got covered in yucky slobber!

When we wanted to run around
there were all these fluffy
things we could chase.
Sometimes it was hard to tell
who was chasing who.
There were a couple of times
I almost got squashed!

Watching the boxes was way more my speed. Sometimes a dog just needs to relax, you know?

My favourite time of day was always dinnertime! One of the machines served us yummy chicken bits.

Then I would always go to the room with the machine that made my smelly poop disappear! Finally I did not have to worry about stepping in it anymore. Boy, that used to really get my paws in a twitch.

One day I was sniffing around
and I found my friend Andi
on the roof. She looked really sad.
I wanted to cheer her up,
but first I needed a snack. Then
I realised she was probably sad
because she needed one too.
I knew I could help!

A few days later I heard a loud noise in the kitchen. The dogs had gone totally wild! They were galloping through the halls, crashing through doors, and popping up all over the place. And they all seemed to be barking at me!

When my pals finally came back
from wherever they had gone,
I smelled a weird scent on them.
If I had not known any better,
I would have thought they
were scared. But I knew better!

I guess I was wrong, though.
Suddenly all my friends were
snarling, and I realised the smell
was from that guy in the uniform.
Somehow he had found me!
Before I knew it we were all
running really fast!

Before I could bark I was back
with that uniformed guy, going
who-knows-where. But this time
I knew exactly what to do . . . I just
did my little collar trick and
I was free!

Then I found my friends, and we got everyone else home safe too. It was a bit scary, but my friends had never let me down before. I knew they would save us.

Finally we were home again.
But all these people followed us.
There were lots of uniforms.
I'd had such a rough day and
I just wanted to sleep!
Then this guy made everyone
quiet down. He must have been
the leader of the pack.

I did not know what he said,
but whatever it was,
he really turned the place around!
Sniff, sniff. Let me tell you –
everything smells a whole lot
better now!

The big guy and the little guy
are both top dogs here now,
just like me.

And there are even more machines
for us to play with. We do not even
have to climb the stairs on our own!

It's still sad when I have to say goodbye to my friends. But I can get behind it when I know they are leaving with great-smelling people!

So the first part of my life was pretty rough. But now things are great! There are people and dogs everywhere – and only good uniforms. But I still love being with my two favourite people most of all.

Well, there are my favourite friends,
so it's time for me to go.
Sniff, sniff. Smells yummy!
I wonder what's for dinner?
Woof! Woof!